THE PUPPY PLACE

BINGO

THE PUPPY PLACE

Don't miss any of these other stories by Ellen Miles!

Angel
Bandit
Barney
Baxter
Bear
Bella
Bentley
Biggie
Bitsy
Bonita
Boomer
Bubbles and Boo
Buddy
Champ
Chewy and Chica
Cocoa
Cody
Cooper
Cuddles
Daisy
Donut
Edward
Flash
Fluffy & Freckles
Gizmo
Goldie
Gus
Honey
Jack
Jake
Kodiak
Liberty
Lily
Lola
Louie
Lucky
Lucy
Maggie and Max
Miki
Mocha
Molly
Moose
Muttley
Nala
Noodle
Oscar
Patches
Princess
Pugsley
Rascal
Rocky
Roxy
Rusty
Scout
Shadow
Snowball
Sparky
Spirit
Stella
Sugar, Gummi, and Lollipop
Sweetie
Teddy
Ziggy
Zig & Zag
Zipper

THE PUPPY PLACE

BINGO

SCHOLASTIC INC.

For Audrey

Cover art by Tim O'Brien
Original cover design by Steve Scott

ISBN 978-1-338-78188-5

10 9 8 7 6 5 4 3 2 1   22 23 24 25 26

Printed in the U.S.A.   40
First printing 2022

CHAPTER ONE

And number twelve is gaining fast, but number eight isn't giving up the race yet, Charles thought, narrating the action to himself. *And now we see the young number three teaming up with number seven to pull way, way ahead!* Charles smiled as he watched fat raindrops streak down the classroom window, near his desk. He was pretending they were racing: whichever one got to the bottom first would win.

"Can you show us, Charles?"

Charles whipped his head toward the front of the room where his teacher, Mr. Mason, stood staring at him. Mr. Mason held out the marker in his hand, inviting Charles to come up to the whiteboard and finish a math problem.

Charles squinted at the board. The numbers made no sense at all. Maybe he needed new glasses. Or maybe, he could imagine Mr. Mason saying, he just needed to pay more attention. "Um," he said.

"How about you, Prema?" Mr. Mason asked, turning to a girl on the other side of the room. She hopped up and, smiling, went to the board. With a few confident strokes she finished the problem, then stood back, looking up at Mr. Mason.

"Exactly," said Mr. Mason. "Does everybody get what Prema did here?"

"Mmm-hmm," Charles murmured, along with the rest of the class. But he wasn't really paying attention anymore. He scooted down in his seat, letting out a sigh. Rainy days at home made him antsy—at least his mom always said so—but rainy days at school made him sleepy.

His classroom felt especially cozy when gray clouds hung low outside but the lights were on inside. The room was quieter than usual; everybody seemed to speak in hushed voices instead of yelling. The smell of damp clothes—they'd played kickball at recess—mixed with all the usual classroom smells.

Charles yawned, then smiled to himself. He was remembering last night with Buddy, his sweet brown puppy. They had curled up on the floor together, watching a movie with the rest of his family (Mom, Dad, and Charles's older sister, Lizzie, and younger brother, the Bean). Charles had scratched the white, heart-shaped spot on Buddy's chest as he tried to keep his eyes open. The movie was longer than he'd expected, and he was having a hard time staying awake. He let out a huge yawn—and then Buddy yawned, too. It had made them all laugh. Charles had always known that yawns were contagious (if you see a person yawn, it makes you want to yawn, too), but he didn't know it happened to dogs, too.

Aw, Buddy. Had there ever been a better puppy in the history of the universe? Now, in the classroom, Charles closed his eyes for a moment, picturing his best pal. Buddy, sleeping all curled up at the foot of Charles's bed. Buddy, chasing a ball Charles threw. Buddy, begging for a treat. Buddy . . .

"Psst!"

Charles felt something hit him on the cheek and saw a rolled-up piece of paper fall to his desk. He looked over at his best friend Sammy, sitting next to him. Sammy raised his eyebrows. "Wake up," he whispered. "You're snoring!"

Charles yawned again and rubbed his eyes. He sat up straighter and tried to follow what Mr. Mason was saying as he scrawled numbers on the whiteboard. The rain spattered on the windows harder now, all the drops melding into one sheet of water. It was really pouring. "Raining cats and dogs," Dad would say.

Why cats and dogs? Why not kittens and puppies? Charles thought. There could never be too many puppies as far as he was concerned. Charles knew he was super lucky that his family, the Petersons, fostered puppies. That is, they took care of puppies who needed help or new homes. Each one stayed only a little while, but Charles fell in love with them all. Big puppies, little puppies, spoiled puppies, sick or hurt puppies—every one of them was special. It was so, so hard to say good-bye to the puppies when they went to their forever homes, but that was how fostering worked.

At least they had kept Buddy. Had there ever really been a question about that? As soon as he had showed up in their lives, the whole family fell in love with him. Buddy was the only foster puppy who had joined the family permanently. Sometimes Charles and Lizzie begged to keep another one of the foster puppies, but their parents always said no. It wasn't fair—but Mom and Dad were firm. If Charles and his siblings wanted to keep fostering puppies, they could only have one full-time puppy of their own. That was the rule.

"All right then," said Mr. Mason, breaking into Charles's daydreams. "You all have a good afternoon and I'll see you tomorrow." He put the cap on his marker and stuck the marker into the jar on his desk.

What? Charles looked over at Sammy, his

eyebrows raised. How had the school day come to an end without him even noticing?

"Oh, and don't forget," Mr. Mason called out, over the noise of everyone jumping up to head to their cubbies. "Robotics club starts today with Ms. Perez."

Sammy threw a fist into the air. "Yes!" he said.

Charles groaned. He and Sammy had been waiting weeks for this club. Ms. Perez was the coolest teacher in school and—well, robotics! Obviously it was going to be amazing.

"Oops," Sammy said. "I forgot you can't go. Bummer."

Charles shoved his stuff into his backpack. "It's okay," he said. It wasn't, but he was trying to convince himself that it was. His mom had volunteered him to spend the next two weeks' worth of after-school time helping out a neighbor. Ms.

Bailey had just had a foot operation and she was going to need someone to run errands, walk her dog, Annie, and take care of little chores. Today was his first day. Mom kept telling him that he was really going to like Ms. Bailey, but that didn't make up for missing robotics.

Charles walked out of school alone since Sammy was on his way to Ms. Perez's classroom. At least it wasn't raining anymore. A weak sun tried to dry out the puddles as Charles trudged down the sidewalk, head down, trying to avoid stepping on any worms.

He heard a familiar car horn and looked up to see his dad waving to him from the front seat of their van. Lizzie was already in her seat.

"Puppy!" Lizzie yelled out the car window, waving him over. "We're getting a new puppy!"

CHAPTER TWO

Charles climbed into the van. "I'm supposed to go to Ms. Bailey's," he said. Of course he wanted to hear all about the puppy, but he didn't want to forget his responsibility, either. He knew that Ms. Bailey's dog, Annie, was waiting for a walk.

Dad nodded. "Right, Ms. Bailey. We'll drop you there right after we pick up Bingo."

"Bingo!" Lizzie shouted. "His name's Bingo. Don't you love it?" She began to sing, at the top of her voice. "There was a farmer had a dog and Bingo was his name-oh!"

Charles put his hands over his ears. Lizzie was

good at a lot of things, but singing was not one of them. Especially when she was this excited. She was practically shouting the words.

"B-I-N-G-O," Lizzie chanted, clapping her hands as she spelled out the word. "Come on, Charles! B-I-N-G-O!"

Where had the peaceful rainy day gone? Charles had to smile. He was excited, too—but he wanted to know more. "Where are we going? What kind of dog is Bingo?" he yelled, so Dad could hear him over Lizzie's racket.

"Your aunt Amanda called me," Dad said, taking one hand off the steering wheel to make a "keep it down" gesture to Lizzie. She quit singing to listen, but she kept bouncing in her seat.

"I guess somebody brought her this puppy—they need to find a home for him and they've heard about us. The story is a little fuzzy so far but we'll find out more when we get there. Amanda will have everyone coming by soon to pick up their dogs, so she wanted us to get there before that."

Aunt Amanda ran a doggy day care named Bowser's Backyard. Charles and Lizzie had both helped out there. It was always a bit of a madhouse, with thirty or more dogs running around playing and barking and shredding toys. Pickup time was especially busy, when all the owners showed up after work to take their dogs home.

"B-I-N-G-O," Lizzie sang under her breath. She sat up straighter. "Did she at least tell you what kind of dog he is?" she asked.

Dad thought for a second. "Some kind of—uh—Chinese something?"

Lizzie bounced in her seat so high that Charles thought she might bang her head on the roof of the van. "A Chinese Crested?" she asked. "Really? Really? That's the one breed I have been dying to meet!"

Charles loved dogs, but his sister—well, she was totally dog-crazy. Lizzie was all about dogs, all the time. She knew all about every breed under the sun. "Are they rare?" he asked. He tried to picture Lizzie's "Dog Breeds of the World" poster, but he couldn't remember anything about a Chinese Crested.

"Very!" said Lizzie. "They're those hairless ones, you know? All they have is a little pompom on the end of their tails and a little pouf on top of their head."

"Hairless?" Dad and Charles exchanged a look in the rearview mirror. "Um, that sounds kinda—" Dad began.

"Gross!" Charles finished.

"No, no, they're really cute," Lizzie said. "And I've always, always wanted to pet one. I mean, I just can't even imagine what that feels like. Is their skin super-soft, or warm, or cool, or what?"

Charles shook his head. A hairless dog? That did not sound cute at all. He could tell Dad was thinking the same. Too bad. Charles had been feeling like maybe a new foster puppy would help make up for missing robotics, but now he wasn't so sure.

"Well, anyway, I guess he needs our help," Dad said. "Your aunt said she really did not want to leave this pup in a kennel overnight at her place. She was in a big rush and couldn't tell me more, but she promised we would understand when we meet him."

Soon enough, Dad pulled into the parking lot of Bowser's Backyard. Charles could see a mob of dogs dashing around in the outdoor play yard, a huge Great Dane leading the pack. They were like a school of fish, darting this way and that but always moving together. Over in the corner were a couple of the shyer dogs, a Dalmatian and some kind of small white fuzzball playing more quietly.

Charles was just about to ask Lizzie what breed the fuzzball was when Aunt Amanda popped out the front door carrying a fluffy black-and-white puppy.

"Oh, wow, look at that one!" he cried. "He's so cute."

The puppy had curly hair, a pointy nose, and a pair of perked-up triangular ears. He wasn't pudgy like a younger pup, but he was still small enough for Aunt Amanda to carry him easily—though he wriggled and squirmed in her arms.

"Hey!" Aunt Amanda waved as they got out of the van. "You made it in record time. Excellent."

"But where's Bingo?" Lizzie asked, looking around.

"Right here!" Aunt Amanda held the puppy up

and gave him a kiss on the nose. "This is Bingo." He wriggled some more and licked her face enthusiastically.

That's me! That's my name!

"But—I thought he was a Chinese Crested," Lizzie said.

Charles couldn't believe it. How could she seem disappointed when Bingo was just about the cutest puppy ever? He reached out slowly to give Bingo a gentle pat. The puppy craned his neck to snuffle at Charles's hand, practically falling out of Aunt Amanda's arms in his eagerness. "Can I hold him?" Charles asked.

"In a sec," said Aunt Amanda. She turned to Lizzie. "First of all, you were right. He is a Chinese Crested. But he's a special type, a—"

“Pompom!” Lizzie cried. “I just remembered. They’re not hairless at all.”

“Thank goodness,” Aunt Amanda said, winking at Charles. He could tell that his aunt shared his feelings about hairless dogs.

Now Lizzie was petting Bingo, too. “He’s pretty cute,” she said, a little grudgingly. “I guess.”

“Pretty cute?” Charles stared at her. He was already head over heels in love with this happy, excited puppy. How could Lizzie not see how adorable he was?

“So, what was the big rush?” Dad asked. “He doesn’t seem hurt or sick or anything.”

“No, he’s fine,” said Aunt Amanda. “The only thing is, he’s almost completely blind.”

CHAPTER THREE

"What?" Charles couldn't believe his ears. He stared up at Aunt Amanda. "What do you mean, blind? You mean he can't see us?" He looked back at Bingo. The puppy snuffled his hand as Charles scritched his cheek. Now Charles could see that Bingo's eyes were a cloudy blue, sort of like new-born puppy's eyes. But Bingo wasn't a baby—he looked as if he might be almost full grown.

Aunt Amanda cleared her throat. "Yup, that's pretty much what I mean. From what I understand he can see a little bit of movement if it's very close to his face and there's enough light. But besides that, Bingo is just about blind."

Charles felt tears spring to his eyes. "That's awful!" he said.

"Well," said Aunt Amanda. "It will make his life a little more challenging, but actually he's a happy little pup, and he doesn't really know the difference."

"Like Sparky," said Lizzie. Charles saw that she had tears in her eyes, too, but she was smiling and nodding.

Aunt Amanda nodded. "Sort of like Sparky," she said. "In fact, Bingo's owner read the article that your mom wrote about Sparky, which is part of the reason she wanted me to ask you to foster Bingo."

Sparky was a puppy the Petersons had fostered. He'd had a bad injury to his leg, and in the end he'd had to have a big operation. Now he got around on three legs—and he was one of the peppiest, happiest pups Charles had ever known.

He played and ran just like any other dog, and never seemed to know that there was any difference. Charles's mom, a newspaper reporter, had written a great article about him after he'd been adopted.

"Bingo just needs love," Charles said softly, stroking the puppy's head.

"Exactly," said Aunt Amanda. "Love and understanding and a little bit of patience." She sighed. "I wish his owner could have understood that. She just couldn't deal with a 'special needs' dog. She said she was afraid to take her eyes off him; he's so high energy that he just zooms around and she was always worried that he'd hurt himself. She felt bad about it, but in the end she decided she couldn't keep him, and she asked me to help. She was embarrassed to ask you herself."

Charles saw Lizzie bite her lip, probably so she wouldn't say something mean about an owner who would give up a dog who needed a different kind of attention. He felt sad about it, too—but more than that, he felt excited. "We can help Bingo," he said. "I know we can. We'll take care of him and find him a home where they won't care whether he can see or not."

"Um," Dad said. "Are you sure, kids? This might mean some extra work for all of us."

"Dad," said Charles. "Look at him. Bingo needs us!"

Dad put out a hand to pet Bingo. Charles could practically see his father's heart melting. Dad was a big softie when it came to babies of every type. "Of course he does," Dad said. "And of course we'll take him."

"Yay!" Charles and Lizzie chorused.

"But how—how did he get blind?" Charles asked his aunt.

"It's probably a genetic problem," said Aunt

Amanda. "That means it was handed down from his mom or dad. Bingo's owner tried to contact the breeder she got him from, but they've closed down and moved away." She shook her head. "It's sad, but there are a lot of breeders out there who don't really know what they're doing."

"We'll take him to Dr. Gibson tomorrow for a checkup," Dad said. The Petersons took all their foster puppies to Dr. Gibson. She was the best vet in the area, and she was always happy to meet the newest pup.

"Good," said Aunt Amanda. "She'll be able to explain more about how and why Bingo has lost his eyesight."

"I still can't believe anyone would give this puppy up," said Charles. "I mean, look at him!" Charles reached out his arms. "Please can I hold him now? He doesn't seem scared of us or anything."

Aunt Amanda nodded. "The thing with a blind dog is that you don't want to surprise him, by grabbing him or doing anything too suddenly," she said. "He can't see you coming, but he can hear you. Be sure and talk to him so he has a sense of what's going on around him."

"Bingo," Charles said softly, "want to come home with us? We'll take really good care of you until we find you the perfect home." Charles felt a little tug in his belly when he said that. He pretty much always wished that the "perfect home" would be with his family—for every foster puppy! "Ready?" he asked as Aunt Amanda put the wriggling, happy Bingo into his arms.

"Oooh," Charles said. "He's so soft." He stuck his nose into the curly fur on Bingo's neck and took a long sniff. "And he smells so good." Bingo wriggled and squirmed and licked Charles's cheeks and his ear and his nose.

You smell pretty good, too!

Lizzie leaned in to take a sniff. "Hi, Bingo," she said, "I'm Lizzie, the big sister. We're going to have fun together." She stroked him carefully and his little tail wagged wildly.

"You two get it; I can see that," said Aunt Amanda. "You can do a little more research on how to take care of a blind pup, but most of it is common sense. Like, you want to make sure he knows where his food and water bowls are, and always keep them in the exact same place so he can find them. It's good that your house is already toddler-proofed because of the Bean, otherwise you might have to put padding on sharp corners and things like that."

Charles and Lizzie were both nodding.

"I told Bingo's owner—former owner—that we would make sure he found a terrific home," Aunt

Amanda added. "I think that made her feel better, and I know it's true." She bent down to nuzzle Bingo's head. "I'll come visit soon, little dude. Meanwhile, have a blast with these peeps!"

Charles carried Bingo out to the van and let Lizzie hold the pup while he climbed in and buckled up. Then he held out his arms. "Give him back," he said. He already felt like Bingo was his special friend.

Lizzie hesitated, but then she must have seen the look on Charles's face. "Oh, all right," she said, nestling the pup into Charles's arms. "We're dropping you off in five minutes, anyway."

Charles gaped at her. "Wha—?" he began. Then he remembered: Today was his first day helping out Ms. Bailey. This was even worse than missing robotics! He wouldn't be there when Lizzie let Bingo into their fenced backyard, the first place they always brought their foster puppies. And he wouldn't get the chance to see how it went when Buddy and Bingo first met. That was always one of the best moments of getting a new foster puppy. Buddy was so terrific with every puppy who came to stay.

"Cheer up," Dad said, meeting his eyes in the rearview mirror. "You'll be home before you know it, and you'll have plenty of Bingo time." He smiled. "Plus, I think you're really going to like—"

"Ms. Bailey," Charles said glumly. "I know, I know. Mom told me that, like, a million times." He kissed the top of Bingo's head. He didn't want to miss a second with this adorable guy, but a promise was a promise.

CHAPTER FOUR

"Door's open! Come on in!"

Charles pushed open the front door of Ms. Bailey's house and stuck his head in, a little unsure. "Hello?" he called.

Even from the first glance, he could see that Ms. Bailey's house was very different from his own, even though they looked a lot alike on the outside—well, except for the fact that her front door was painted purple with red trim, her house was yellow, and her shutters were bright blue. Inside, her house was exploding with color and full of interesting things to look at. Like, right in the front hall, instead of a row of shoes on the floor and coats on hooks like at his house, there was a tall glass-fronted case full of—what? Charles leaned closer. Rocks and feathers and—he gasped a little—a tiny skeleton. Like, from a mouse or something. And a bigger bone that looked like it had once been part of something much, much bigger—a moose?

"Charles? Is that you?" a voice called.

"It's me," he answered. "Hi, Ms. Bailey."

"Margaret, please! I'm in the living room. Come on in—no need to take off your shoes or anything."

Charles found his way to the living room, where Ms. Bailey sat on a huge dark-green couch, surrounded by piles of books, newspapers, and magazines. This room was also like no other living room Charles had ever seen. The walls were painted deep red and filled with paintings of birds, animals, and plants. A row of bird's nests lined the fireplace mantel, and an ivy plant sent tendrils all around the room. A huge window looked out onto Ms. Bailey's backyard, which looked more like a woodland park—all overgrown bushes and twining vines hanging from full-grown trees—than like the close-clipped lawn and flower gardens at his own house.

Ms. Bailey herself was also pretty interesting to look at, dressed in a bright red kimono decorated with dragons. She had wild, curly gray hair and a broad smile. She waved him over. "Welcome, Charles! And really, call me Margaret. So great that you can help me out!" she said. She pointed to her foot, which she had propped up on a rustic-looking stool carved from what looked like a tree stump. "I'm stuck sitting here for at least a week before I can even limp around on crutches."

Charles stood next to the couch, feeling a little self-conscious. What was he supposed to do, exactly?

"Well, the first thing is to get Annie out," said Ms. Bailey as if she'd read his mind. She patted a mound of blankets next to her on the couch, and Charles saw a furry nose poke out to snuffle her hand. "Annie's getting older, and she's a little deaf, and she doesn't need a whole lot of exercise—but she does like to go out and check on things in the backyard now and then—don't you, my good girl?" Ms. Bailey bent over to kiss her dog's grizzled gray face. "She was out earlier today—my niece Audrey is also helping out. She and Annie are best pals since Audrey house-sits for me whenever I'm away."

"I can walk Annie," said Charles. That was one thing he knew he could do—he was used to dogs. "Where's her leash?"

"Hanging by the back door," said Ms. Bailey. "Though you'll hardly need it to take her out back. She knows her way around, and her running-off days are far behind her."

Charles patted his leg. "Want to go out, Annie?" he asked, pitching his voice a little louder so she could hear him. At the sound of her name, she swung her head up to look at him, then slowly, carefully, pushed herself up and off the couch. She stood next to Ms. Bailey for a moment, looking uncertain.

"It's okay, girl," she said. "I'll be fine. You can go with Charles." She laughed. "Annie is like my nurse," she said. "She knows I'm not my usual self, and I guess she's a bit worried. She's never more than a few inches away from me these days." She ruffled the dog's ears. "Go on, sweetie," she said. She pointed Charles toward the back of the house.

Annie trotted after Charles, following him into the kitchen where he found her leash hanging on a hook. The kitchen was painted bright taxi-cab yellow, and the shelves were lined with bowls in red, yellow, and orange. Cheerful daisy-printed curtains hung at the window over the sink. Charles smiled. It was like the room was filled with sunshine, even on this dreary day. "Okay, Annie," he said, clipping the old dog's leash to her collar. "Let's see what's happening outside."

He followed Annie through the backyard, waiting as she stopped to sniff each bush and plant along the winding stone path through what seemed like an overgrown jungle. Charles saw birds flitting through the bushes and heard a squirrel chattering at them from high up in a tree. Annie glanced up but didn't seem to need to chase it like Buddy would have. She just plodded along, her big old head swaying and her tail wagging contentedly. "You really are a good girl," Charles said. The leash was loose in his hand; he could tell that Ms. Bailey was right: Annie hardly needed it.

When they came back inside, Annie climbed right back up onto the couch to curl up next to her "patient." Ms. Bailey asked Charles to make her a cup of tea. "You can use the electric kettle," she said, "and look in the drawer next to the sink for my hibiscus blend. I think you'll enjoy that one, too."

"Hi—what?" Charles asked.

"It's a dried flower," said Ms. Bailey. "I mix it with some other herbs, like wild mint and lemon verbena. It's beautifully pink and very calming."

She might as well have been speaking another language, but Charles nodded. Mom had mentioned that Ms. Bailey knew a lot about something called "wild-crafting"—knowing how to find herbs and other food that grew in the wild. He went to make the tea and found the one she was talking about in a whole drawerful of jars that had handwritten labels, mostly words he'd never heard of before.

When he came back into the living room, he found Ms. Bailey polishing a wooden spoon, adding drops of oil from a small bottle as she rubbed the smooth, glowing wood with a rag.

"That's cool," he said.

"Thanks!" she said. "I made it." She handed the spoon to Charles in exchange for her mug of tea, and he took a closer look.

"It's beautiful," he said. He'd never seen anything quite like it. It looked like it was still part of the tree that the wood came from.

"You can make one, too," she said. "I'll teach you. Now, sit down and tell me all about this new puppy you picked up today. I can tell that you're bursting with the news." She pointed to a cozy armchair next to the couch, and Charles sat. He was beginning to have the feeling that his parents were right. He liked Ms. Bailey—Margaret—a lot.

CHAPTER FIVE

"Where is he? Where's Bingo?"

"Hello to you, too," said Charles's mom, laughing. She grabbed him to give him a hug as he ran by. "Take it easy," she said as she gave him a squeeze. "Bingo is still getting used to everything here."

Charles hugged her back, then squirmed away and headed out to the yard, where Bingo and Buddy were playing together.

"Are they getting along?" Charles asked, sitting down on the deck stairs, next to his sister.

"Uh, you tell me!" Lizzie said. "Look at them go!"

Charles laughed as he watched Bingo chase Buddy around the yard. If you didn't know better, you'd never guess that Bingo was blind. He ran just as fast as Buddy did and managed to dodge most of the things in his way. When he somersaulted into a bush or skidded into a flower bed, he got up, shook himself off, and started running again. It reminded Charles of the way the Bean would toddle around, fall down on his butt, cry for one second, then start toddling around again. "How does he do it when he can't even see?" Charles asked.

"I walked him around the yard first and tried to help him understand where everything was," said Lizzie. "The swing set, the rosebushes—he seemed to catch on right away."

Buddy dashed up to say hello to Charles, with Bingo tearing along right behind him. "Hey,

Buddy," said Charles, ruffling his puppy's ears. "Hey, Bingo."

Bingo scrambled right up into Charles's lap and started to lick his face and nibble on his nose.

Hi, hi, hi! Great to see you again!

Charles laughed. "It's me, Charles. Remember? I'm a friend. But I guess you already know that." He could feel Bingo's heart beating hard as he petted the excited little pup. "Has he learned his way around inside yet?" he asked Lizzie. "Let's show him where everything is."

"You can do that," Lizzie said. "I have to go take care of my clients." Lizzie had a dog-walking business that kept her busy on weekday afternoons.

Charles carried Bingo inside and set him down in the living room. "Okay, Bingo, let's explore this room." Bingo took off at a full gallop, smashed into the leg of the coffee table, and sat back on his butt.

Oof. Okay, now I know where at least one of the hard things is.

"Oh, Bingo," said Charles. "Are you okay?" Luckily, the coffee table legs had padding on them, to keep the Bean from banging himself. By the time Charles got closer, Bingo was already up and shaking himself off. Next, he headed for the couch. Charles crawled after him and gently removed the puppy's paw when Bingo tried climbing up.

"Uh-uh," said Charles. "No dogs on the couch—well, at least unless Mom's not around." Charles waited while Bingo sniffed his way around the couch. "No, no," said Charles, when Bingo tried again to climb up. "No couch." Then, when all four of Bingo's feet were on the floor, "Good dog!"

Bingo took off running again, until he crashed into the big recliner near the fireplace. This time, he bounced right up again and put a paw up on the chair, snuffling.

I know this person! And I like him, too. I want to be close to him.

"Yup, that's Dad's chair," said Charles. "Dad is the guy you met before. I guess you remember his smell. But you don't get to go up on his chair." Carefully, Charles steered Bingo away from the chair.

"That's great, Charles. Nice and gentle."

Charles looked up to see Mom standing in the kitchen doorway, watching him. He smiled at her.

"Bingo's really smart," he said. "I can tell already. He learns fast."

"He's pretty wild, too. Maybe a little too confident! He's had to figure out a lot in his young life," Mom said. She held up two fingers. "Dad just went to pick up the Bean from day care. Dinner in two minutes, when they're back," she said. "All you good dogs are invited."

At dinner, Charles told everyone about his time with Ms. Bailey. "She seems really cool," he said. "Like, she's done all kinds of adventures, from hiking in the Grand Canyon to working on a fishing boat in Alaska." Charles had asked Margaret about some of the pictures on her walls, and she'd told him some wild stories.

"That's the least of it!" said his dad. "I remember her tall tales, from back when she used to volunteer as an EMT."

Charles knew that an EMT was an emergency

medical technician. Charles's dad was an EMT, and a firefighter, too. Somehow it didn't surprise Charles that someone like Margaret would be good at helping people when they were sick or hurt.

"Did she tell you she used to work in Antarctica, at one of the research stations?" Dad asked. "And that she once rode her bicycle from Ireland to India?"

Charles's jaw dropped. "Is that even possible?" he asked.

"Anything's possible for Margaret," said his mom. "I once did an interview with her and found out that when she was twenty-three she was the world champion in a certain kind of water-skiing. I spent a whole afternoon talking to her, at the yurt she lives in over the summer."

"What? What is a yurt?" Lizzie asked.

"It's a type of round tent," Mom said. "It's used

by Mongolian nomads is what she told me. It was really cozy and sweet."

Charles looked back and forth at his parents, listening. Margaret was even more amazing than he'd realized. He couldn't wait to tell Sammy about her. Margaret might even be cooler than robotics!

"She loves dogs, too," said Charles.

"Maybe you could bring Bingo over to meet her," Mom said. "We've got to find some ways to burn off some of that crazy energy of his."

Charles shook his head. "I told her all about Bingo, and she's dying to see him, but she doesn't want me to bring him over. She says Annie can be a little cranky with younger dogs. And she says Annie is old enough that she deserves a peaceful life."

Mom rolled her eyes as something banged into

the table, making it wobble. Bingo and Buddy were under the table, wrestling with each other and bumping against everybody's legs. "I think I know just how Annie feels," she said.

CHAPTER SIX

"Gah! He's adorable!" Dr. Gibson put her hands up to her cheeks, eyes wide, when she got her first look at Bingo.

It was Saturday morning, and Charles and his dad had brought Bingo to meet the vet. Lizzie was busy volunteering at the animal shelter, and Mom and the Bean were running errands. Charles was glad it was just him and Dad; Bingo could get pretty keyed up, and it was better to keep things quiet. That was easier with fewer people.

"What a cutie pie," Dr. Gibson went on as she picked Bingo up to set him on her exam table.

She moved slowly, so as not to surprise him. "You can stand right here, Charles, and keep your hand on Bingo while I listen to his heart and check him out."

Charles went up to the table and stood close to Bingo's head, petting him and scritching him between the ears. Bingo squirmed at first, but when he felt Dr. Gibson's gentle hands he stood still and let the vet touch him all over.

She put her stethoscope to Bingo's chest, talking softly to him as she moved. "Just gonna have a quick listen," she murmured. She was silent for a moment. Then she nodded. "Good strong heartbeat," she said. "And he looks healthy and well-fed. Seems like the main issue is his eyesight."

"Why would a puppy so young be losing his vision?" Dad asked. "I mean, I know older dogs sometimes go blind, but a puppy?"

Dr. Gibson nodded. "I'd have to do more testing," she said, "but I'm almost sure that Bingo has what's called Progressive Retinal Atrophy. It's a genetic condition," she explained to Charles. She peered into Bingo's milky blue eyes, one at a time, then moved her fingers in front of his face. "See how he doesn't blink or pull away when I do that?" she asked. "He really can't see my hand, even when it's moving."

She shook her head. "It's a shame," she said. "But most dogs who have this lose their vision slowly, so they adapt—they get used to it over time."

"That explains the way he runs around like a wild thing," said Dad. "He's fearless!" He told her about the way Bingo had explored their house—at top speed!

"Better keep a baby gate at the top of the stairs," said Dr. Gibson.

"We already do, for the Bean," said Dad. "Fortunately, the whole house is pretty toddler-proofed."

"Can Bingo have an operation or something?" Charles had stayed awake wondering about that last night. He would have done anything to help Bingo be able to see.

Dr. Gibson sighed. "There's really nothing that can be done. The good news is that as you can already tell, he'll manage just fine. With some help from you, he'll start to calm down a bit and take his time as he's learning about a new place."

"I just wish he could see," Charles said. He still didn't think it was fair at all.

Dr. Gibson put her hand on Charles's shoulder. "You know," she told him, "some people say that blind dogs see with their hearts."

Charles felt tears come to his eyes. That was

perfect for Bingo! The little black-and-white pup loved everybody he met—and everybody he met loved him, both people and dogs.

"Buddy doesn't even seem to notice that there's anything different about Bingo," Charles told the vet.

"Exactly," said Dr. Gibson. "Dogs don't pay attention to things like that. They'll treat him just the same, and so should you—with a little extra care to help him learn his way around—safely."

"Can you explain how we do that?" Dad asked. "I'm the one who'll be caring for him when the kids are at school. I'm on leave from the fire-house this week—I was just planning to get some stuff done around the house, so I'll have plenty of time."

By now, Bingo was getting squirmy. He couldn't seem to stay still for long. Dr. Gibson lifted him off her exam table and put him on the floor.

Immediately, he took off running—but his paws slipped out from under him on the shiny tiled floor. He scrabbled up and started out again, at a slower pace. "See how fast he learns?" Dr. Gibson said. Bingo sniffed all around—at the cabinets, at the scale, and at Dr. Gibson's ankles.

Okay, I think I get it. This place is all hard edges, but the person is nice.

"One way you can help is to keep his food and water dishes in the exact same place every day," said Dr. Gibson.

"That's what Aunt Amanda told us!" said Charles. "What else?"

"I did some research on this when I heard you were bringing in a blind puppy," said Dr. Gibson. "It seems like some people use smells or sounds to help the puppy find his way. Like, you could put a little peppermint oil on places where he's not allowed to go. Then you teach him that the peppermint smell means 'no.' You can also get him toys that smell good—like a chew toy that smells like bacon—so he can find his own toys easily. And you can train him using sound, like you could clap your hands when it's time for him to pay attention to you."

Dad was taking notes on his phone. "Uh-huh," he said. "Got it. We can do some more research, too. We've got a lot to learn."

Now Bingo was scratching at the door, whining a little under his breath. "I think somebody's ready to go," said Charles. He picked up the end of Bingo's leash.

"And just try to keep things as calm as possible around the house," finished Dr. Gibson as she walked them out to the door. "Bingo really needs to learn how to settle down, before he gets hurt."

Dad laughed. "Not too many people would call our house calm," he said. "But we do understand puppies. We'll do our best."

CHAPTER SEVEN

Later that day, Charles kissed Bingo for the eighty-billionth time and headed off to Margaret's. He couldn't wait to tell her about all the new things Bingo had already learned, like the best spot for daytime napping (in the front hall, when the sun came in the windows), how to get Mom to give him a treat (basically, tilt his head and put one paw up, looking super cute), and the quickest route to the back door, for when it was time to pee.

"He's just so smart," Charles told Sammy, who had begged to come along to Margaret's with him. "He might be the smartest puppy we ever fostered."

"Don't let Buddy hear you say that," said Sammy.

"Well, of course Buddy is the smartest and cutest and best," Charles said. "But Bingo is right up there. And the two of them get along so well. It's like they're brothers."

"You want to keep him, don't you?" Sammy asked. "You know your parents will never say yes to that."

"I know," said Charles. He kicked at a rock on the sidewalk. "But I can still dream about it, can't I?"

Margaret's house was only a few blocks away, but by the time they got there Charles already missed Bingo so much that his stomach hurt. "I just wish she would let me bring him over," he said as they climbed Margaret's front steps. He knocked lightly on the door, then let himself in, the way Margaret had told him to do.

"Hello?" he called.

"In here," Margaret called back. "Did you bring your friend?" She smiled when she saw Sammy follow Charles into the room. "Hi, Sammy," she said. "I'm Margaret, and this is Annie. She's ready to go out back, but then I want you to come in and tell me all about robotics club."

Sammy looked at Charles and raised his eyebrows. Charles nodded. "I told Margaret about that when I asked if you could come," he said. "She's really interested."

"Okay," said Sammy. "But I want to hear about the time you faced down a grizzly bear in Alaska, too."

"Deal!" said Margaret, clapping her hands.

Charles and Sammy took Annie outside. She wandered through the yard, stopping here and there for a sniff and a pee. She paused at the gate that led out of the yard, scratched at it, and looked up at Charles. "Are you bored with the yard, Annie?" Charles asked. "Maybe we can take you for a longer walk. I'll ask Margaret."

"Sure," she said, when they came back inside and Charles told her what Annie had done. "She must be missing her neighborhood walks. I didn't even think of that. Let's have some lunch, and then you can take her out."

Charles went into the kitchen and, following the directions Margaret had given him, made three cheese sandwiches. He put each one on a plate, added a handful of chips, and brought them out to Margaret and Sammy.

". . . and that's how I lived to tell the story," Margaret was saying to Sammy, finishing her grizzly bear tale, the one Charles had heard the day before. It involved tossing the bear a giant salmon she'd just caught and then running like mad for her truck. "Now, tell us all about robotics."

Sammy told them all about the first meeting of robotics club. "Basically we just learned about what robots are and what they can do," he said. "Which is, like, just about anything. They can do operations, and make cars, and plant crops . . ."

"But can they give hugs?" Margaret asked, giving Annie a squeeze and slipping her a potato chip. "Or whittle a spoon?"

"Well, no," said Sammy.

"I'm just kidding," Margaret said. "Sort of. I think robots are incredibly cool, and I've been wanting to learn more about them. But there are always going to be things that only humans can do, right?"

"Right," said Sammy. He told them that the club project was going to be building a robot that could pick up marbles and put them into a container. "Pretty simple, but cool. There's going to be a demonstration night where we can invite our friends and family," he told Margaret. "Maybe by then you'll be able to walk, and you can come."

"I'd love that!" Margaret pushed herself up into a better sitting position. "I'm already getting pretty tired of this couch, I can tell you that. I can understand how Annie feels, cooped up in the house and yard. Why don't you boys take her for a longer walk?" She reached for her book. "I'll be fine here on my own."

"Are you sure?" Charles asked. He'd been getting the feeling that a big part of his job with Margaret was just keeping her company.

"I'm sure," she said, smiling at him. "Go, Annie!" She had to push the big dog off the couch. Annie did not like to be too far away from Margaret, that was obvious. Annie climbed down slowly, then looked back at Margaret. "I said, I'm sure!" Margaret said, laughing. "I tell you, it's like having a full-time nurse with this one around." She ruffled Annie's ears. "Have a nice walk, sweetie," she said.

Charles clipped on Annie's leash and he and Sammy headed off down the block. "You were right about Margaret," Sammy said. "She's so cool. I wonder what she's going to do next."

"She's always looking at maps," Charles said. "I think she said something about going to Madagascar?" Annie walked along next to Charles. She seemed happy to be out of the yard: she wagged her tail as she walked and stopped to sniff every few steps. She wasn't going to win any speed prizes—Sammy and Charles had to walk extra slowly so she could keep up—but that didn't matter.

Just as they turned the corner, Charles heard Lizzie calling his name. "Hey, Charles!" she shouted. "Look who's out for a walk!" She pointed to Bingo, out in front of her on a leash. The puppy was veering from side to side, sniffing everything and practically bouncing with excitement. He carried his new bacon-scented toy in his mouth.

Annie perked up. She pulled in front of Charles and stared at Bingo, her ears alert and her head cocked. She let out a deep "woof."

Bingo stopped in his tracks, head tilted in her direction. He dropped his toy.

Before Charles could stop her, Annie lunged toward the black-and-white pup, pulling her leash right out of his hands.

CHAPTER EIGHT

"Annie! No!" shouted Charles.

"She's going after Bingo," Sammy said. He ran to grab her leash, but she was too quick. The leash flicked out of his fingers as he tumbled to the ground, banging his knees. "Ow!" he yelled.

Charles groaned. "Oh, no," he said, remembering what Margaret had said about keeping Annie away from the puppy. This was a disaster.

"Bingo!" Lizzie said, stepping forward and bending down as if to scoop the puppy up out of Annie's way.

Time seemed to slow down, but when they

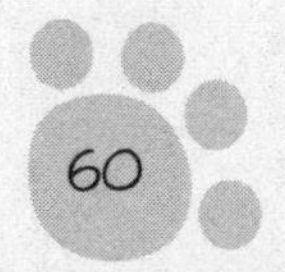

talked about it later they all agreed that it had all probably happened in a matter of three seconds.

Number One: Annie pulled away from Charles.

Number Two: She pounced on Bingo's toy.

And then, the very surprising Number Three that happened before any of them could move: Annie carried the toy to Bingo and gently laid it at his paws.

"Wait, what?" Sammy asked, rubbing his knee.

Charles stared in disbelief as the big black Lab nudged the toy closer until Bingo felt it and bent his head to pick it up again. Charles's heart was thumping. If the puppy picked up the toy, would Annie lunge at it—or at Bingo? She was three times his size and he didn't stand a chance if she wanted to fight him over a bacon-scented chew toy.

Now Lizzie did pick up Bingo. "I'm not sure I

trust her," she said, looking at Annie. "Didn't Margaret say she could be cranky with puppies?"

But Bingo squirmed in her arms, struggling to get down.

I trust her! I like her! She found my toy and brought it back to me.

Lizzie looked at Charles, eyebrows raised. "He really wants to be with her," she said. "What do you think?"

Charles shrugged. "I don't hear Annie growling," he said. "And she's always seemed really gentle and sweet, at least around me."

"Plus, her tail is wagging," Sammy added, from where he still sat on the sidewalk, rubbing his knee.

Sure enough, the big dog stood calmly, looking

up at Bingo with a doggie grin on her face. Her tail wagged slowly as she gave another low, deep "woof."

This time, Bingo squirmed right out of Lizzie's arms and jumped down to meet his new friend. He wagged his tail double-time as he and Annie sniffed each other.

Thanks for fetching my toy! You're a pal.

"They seem fine together," said Lizzie. "Should we take them to our yard so they can play off-leash for a little while?"

Charles paused. Margaret had asked him not to bring Bingo over to her house. She hadn't said anything at all about whether he could take Annie to his house. "Sure," he said, after a moment. It was obvious that the two dogs were getting along perfectly. Wasn't it a good thing for Bingo to meet other dogs?

He and Sammy followed Lizzie back to the house, and they all went straight to the backyard. Lizzie let Bingo off his leash, then went in to ask Dad not to let Buddy out while Annie and Bingo got to know each other.

Charles unsnapped Annie's leash, too. She shook herself off, her collar tags jangling, then lay down to roll in the green grass. She made happy grunting noises as she wriggled and rolled.

Bingo stood still, head cocked. Charles thought he must be trying to figure out what Annie was doing. Then he lay down, too, and wriggled, and made happy noises.

When she was done, Annie stood up and shook off again. Bingo did the same.

That felt good!

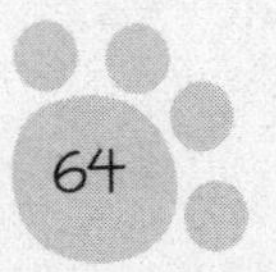

"Look, he copies everything she does," said Sammy.

"So cute," said Lizzie, who had come back out.

Bingo began to jump at Annie, trying to get her to play. He pawed at her and nipped her ears, whining and yipping.

Charles bit his lip, waiting to see if Annie would growl or bark at the pesky puppy. Maybe this whole thing had been a really bad idea. What if Annie bit Bingo? It would all be his fault if Bingo got hurt. Margaret had told him that Annie wasn't always nice to puppies.

But Annie didn't bite. She just put one big paw out and set it on Bingo's back. The little pup calmed down right away.

"Whoa!" said Lizzie. "She's being so patient and gentle."

"Good girl, Annie," said Charles. He watched as Annie got to her feet and began to stroll around the yard, with Bingo sticking right next to her. She nudged him gently away when he was about to run into a rosebush, and waited while he sniffed at some new yellow flowers that had bloomed that morning.

"They get along great," said Sammy.

"They really do," said Charles. "I almost hate to take Annie home, but Margaret's going to wonder where we are." He called Annie, and she trotted over with Bingo at her heels. Charles clipped on her leash. "Say good-bye, Annie," he said. He felt relieved that the meeting had gone well. It was better to end on a good note than wait for something bad to happen.

"Have a nice walk, old girl?" Margaret asked Annie, when they got back. She scritched Annie's ears as the dog climbed back up onto the couch to settle in.

"I think she did," said Charles. He looked at

Sammy and they exchanged a tiny smile. They had decided it might be better not to tell Margaret what had happened. After all, nothing really *had* happened, had it?

CHAPTER NINE

Later, after dinner, Charles and Lizzie and the Bean sat out on the deck with Popsicles, watching Buddy and Bingo play.

"Look at him go!" said Charles. "Bingo really is fearless."

"Ouch!" said Lizzie as Bingo slammed into the swing set. "And maybe that's not always a great thing."

"Bingo is fast!" said the Bean. "Go, Bingo, go!" He pumped his fist and dropped his grape Popsicle. Buddy dashed right over to lick up the sweet mess. The Bean looked surprised for a moment, then screwed up his face as if he was about to start howling.

Quickly, Charles handed over his orange Popsicle. "Orange is even better," he told his little brother.

Bingo ran over to find out what was happening. He pawed at the Bean's knee, his head cocked.

Is everything okay? Don't be upset. Want to snuggle?

Buddy ignored everything and lapped even more quickly at the sweet purple puddle next to the Bean.

Charles laughed. "If that was Annie, she'd probably share with Bingo," he said. "But Buddy's, like, 'this is my Popsicle!'"

At the sound of Annie's name, Bingo's ears

went up. He swiveled his head as if listening for her footsteps. Then he went down the deck stairs to the spot where he and Annie had been lying together earlier that day. He sniffed all around, then curled up and lay down.

"They sure did get along great," said Lizzie. "What did Margaret think about it?"

Charles looked down at his feet. "We—uh—we didn't tell her," he admitted.

Lizzie raised her eyebrows.

"I thought she might get mad at me," said Charles, even though—now that he thought about it—that wasn't how Margaret was. "I like helping her and hearing her stories and everything. What if she fired me?"

Lizzie laughed. "It's not like an actual job, Charles," she said, in her annoying know-it-all big sister way.

"Whatever," Charles grumbled. He went down the stairs to sit next to Bingo on the grass. He knew he'd been wrong not to tell Margaret—but it was too late now. He petted Bingo's soft, springy curls. "If she would just meet you, she'd love you," he told the little pup.

The next day, Charles headed to Margaret's after school. He planned to confess everything as soon as he arrived—but he forgot all about it when he saw how upset Margaret was. "I think Annie's sick," she told him, when he came in. "She's been moping around all day, and when my niece Audrey came this morning, Annie barely wanted to go out. She wouldn't even eat her breakfast! I'm not sure that's ever happened before." She stroked Annie's big head as the dog lay next to her, chin on her paws. Annie looked up at Charles, and for a moment she perked up, cocking her head and sniffing the air. Then she let out a sigh and put her head back down.

"Maybe she's just tired," said Charles. He thought of the way Annie had played in the yard yesterday, galumphing around with Bingo trotting at her side. Maybe they had worn her out.

"I hope that's all it is," said Margaret. "But what if she's sick? What if there's something really wrong? I can't stand the thought of losing my girl."

Charles wanted to tell Margaret how happy Annie had been with Bingo yesterday, but now he was really worried that he'd done something wrong. What if it had been too tiring for her to play with a puppy? What if he'd made her sick?

The truth was, Charles didn't think that was it at all. In fact, he thought it was the opposite. He thought that maybe Annie missed Bingo. There was only one way for him to find out if he was right.

"I'll take her for a walk again," he suggested. "Maybe she's just feeling bored because of being stuck at home all the time."

As soon as they left Margaret's house, Annie perked up. She began to speed-walk down the sidewalk, towing Charles toward the spot where they'd met Bingo the day before. "Uh-huh," Charles said as he trotted along after her. "I thought so. You miss that little guy, don't you? You miss Bingo."

At the sound of her new friend's name, Annie wagged her tail. She looked down the street, scanning the sidewalk with her ears on alert. Then, suddenly, she let out that deep "woof." She stopped and stared, quivering a little with excitement. She wagged her tail harder and planted both front paws in a play bow.

Charles followed her glance. Sure enough, there was Bingo, towing Lizzie toward them as fast as his little legs would go. He must have heard Annie's bark.

The two dogs had a happy reunion, with plenty of joyful tail wagging and sniffing. Lizzie and Charles laughed as they watched.

"These two are crazy about each other," Lizzie said. "It's obvious."

Charles agreed. "They're good for each other, too. Annie calms Bingo down and keeps him safe, and I think Bingo makes Annie feel young again. I wish Margaret could see them together."

"It would be great for both dogs if you could bring Bingo over there to visit," said Lizzie.

Charles nodded, feeling miserable. "I know," he said. "But how am I going to explain to Margaret that they've already met? Why didn't I tell her so right away?" He groaned. "I really messed up."

Annie stopped sniffing Bingo for a moment and came over to comfort Charles. He felt her warm breath as she snuffled at his hand, and he scritched her between the ears as he thought.

"You know what you're going to have to do, right?" Lizzie asked. "You're going to have to tell Dad. He'll help fix things."

CHAPTER TEN

Charles and Lizzie walked back to their house with both dogs. Lizzie stayed out in the yard with Bingo and Annie while Charles went inside to talk to Dad.

"I didn't exactly lie to Margaret," he said as he explained the mess he'd gotten himself into.

"But you didn't exactly tell the truth, either, right?" Dad asked. He patted the couch next to him and Charles sat down. He felt better as soon as Dad put an arm around his shoulders.

"Nope," said Charles, shaking his head.

"There's really only one thing to do," said Dad.

"You're going to have to tell Margaret everything, apologize, and hope she understands. The sooner you do it, the better." He looked Charles in the eye. "Can you do that?"

"I—I'm not sure," said Charles.

"Tell you what," said Dad, reaching for his phone. "I'll get things started, and then you can take over. Fair?"

Charles nodded.

"You'll feel better as soon as it's all out in the open," Dad said. "I promise." He scrolled through his contacts. "There she is, Margaret! I thought I still had her in there from when she was on our EMT squad." He dialed and put the phone to his ear. "Margaret? Paul Peterson here. Charles is really enjoying getting to know you." He listened. "Well, that's nice to hear," he said, beaming at Charles. "We think he's a pretty wonderful kid, too." He took a deep breath and dove in. "But there's something he needs to tell you, and he and I are both hoping you'll understand."

Dad held the phone out to Charles, raising his eyebrows. "Ready?" he mouthed.

Charles wasn't, but he took the phone. "Hi, Margaret," he said, talking quickly to get it over with faster. "I'm over at my house. Um, with Annie, of course. She met our foster puppy Bingo yesterday and then again today. They really, really like each other, they get along great, and Annie wasn't cranky at all and she really helps make him calmer and he cheers her up and . . ." He paused, knowing that he was talking too much, too fast. He took a big breath.

Dad nudged him and mouthed, "Apology!"

Charles nodded. "Anyway I'm really really sorry I didn't tell you. It was only because—because I don't know." He stopped short. He didn't want to say that he'd been afraid to make her mad since he knew that was silly. Suddenly, he realized that Margaret was talking. "What?" he asked. "Sorry, I didn't hear you."

"I said, I guess you'd better bring him over," Margaret said again.

"What?" Charles asked again. For a second, he wondered if Margaret meant he should bring Dad over. "You mean—bring Bingo?"

Margaret laughed. "Of course! I've been dying to meet him, and from what you say there really isn't any reason to keep him away from Annie."

"We'll be right there!" Charles said, grinning at his dad and giving him a big thumbs-up.

Dad and Lizzie came along as Charles headed back to Margaret's. He held Annie's leash, and Lizzie held Bingo's. The two dogs trotted along in front, with Annie gently guiding Bingo this way and that to help him avoid a tree, a mailbox, and a fire hydrant.

"Wow, it's a party!" said Margaret, when they arrived. "Welcome, everyone." Annie went straight to the couch and climbed up to be next to Margaret. Bingo followed, just as he'd followed her down the street.

"Uh—" Charles began, wondering if that was okay with Margaret.

"It's fine," she said as if reading his mind. "Hello, Bingo!" She reached out gently to let him sniff her hand.

Bingo didn't seem shy at all with Margaret. He wagged his little tail as he climbed right into her lap, craning his neck up to lick her face.

Hi! I already know that you're a friend—
because my friend Annie loves you!

“Wow,” said Margaret. “I know you said he was cute, but I could never have imagined he was *this* cute.” She petted Bingo and cooed his name. “Bingo, Bingo. I hear you and my Annie are good friends,” she said softly.

“It’s even more than that,” said Lizzie. “Annie is like—like his guide dog! She seems to know exactly how to calm Bingo down and keep him safe.”

“And Bingo knows how to bring out Annie’s playful side,” Charles added. “She acts like a puppy around him.”

Dad picked up a map from the stack on a side table. “Where to next?” he asked Margaret. “I’m sure you’re more than ready for your next adventure.”

“I am,” Margaret said. “But I have a feeling it will be a very different type of adventure. I’ve had time to think about it while I’ve been stuck on this couch, and I’ve decided that it’s time to settle down a bit, enjoy my life right here at home. I might even get some chickens."

Dad raised his eyebrows. "No more epic bike rides? No more wilderness expeditions?"

"Oh, maybe one or two," said Margaret. "But I think I've realized that pretty much everything I've been chasing after is right here at home. There's plenty to learn and do without going half-way around the world." She flicked a hand at the pile of maps. "Plus, when I thought Annie might be sick—well, I don't want to miss another precious day with my old girl."

"You know, I think your old girl might like having a young friend join her household," Charles heard the words come out of his mouth before he'd even really thought them through. But it was true! What better home could the Petersons possibly find for Bingo?

"I think you might be right," said Margaret,

smiling down at Annie and Bingo, who now lay curled up next to each other on the couch. She reached out to scritch Annie between the ears, and Bingo pushed his head up into her hand.

Me, too! I need some petting!

"Bingo agrees," said Lizzie.

Dad grinned. "We all do," he said. "I mean, look at them. How could you separate these two?"

"Well, then, I guess it's settled," said Margaret. "Welcome home, Bingo!" She leaned down to kiss the puppy's head.

Charles felt happy tears come to his eyes. He was glad for Bingo, and glad for Annie—and glad for himself! Now he would get to see Bingo every time he visited Margaret.

PUPPY TIPS

I've always wanted to write about a blind puppy, but the right story had not come to me. As soon as I started to think about a puppy who met another dog who could be his "seeing-eye" dog, or at least a helper, this story began to come together. It was so interesting to do research about blind puppies and dogs and how they learn to cope with not being able to see. It seems that, like Bingo, most blind dogs do just fine with a little extra love and care. Now that you've read about Bingo, you'll know what to do if you ever meet a blind puppy or dog: speak gently, move slowly, and let them know you're a friend.

Dear Reader,

One of the fun things about being a writer is that you get to come up with characters and name them whatever you want. I named Margaret Bailey after my grandmother, who was quite an adventurer and who knew everything about nature. I named her niece Audrey after my friend's granddaughter, who also loves nature and animals—and I named Annie after Audrey's dog! (Audrey also has chickens, but that's a whole other story.)

Yours from the Puppy Place,

Ellen Miles

THE PUPPY PLACE

DON'T MISS THE NEXT PUPPY PLACE ADVENTURE!

Here's a peek at BARKLEY

"Over here, Buddy!" Lizzie clapped her hands and watched, smiling, as her little brown puppy looked up, spotted her, and dashed toward her, leaving behind a cluster of other dogs in all different sizes and shapes.

"What a good boy," Lizzie said as Buddy sat panting in front of her. She popped a liver treat into his mouth and he gobbled it down, wagging his tail. Then he grinned up at her and wagged his tail even harder. You didn't have to be able to speak Dog to know what he was saying.

"You want more treats?" Lizzie asked. She laughed. "Maybe later. Go on and play." She waved him away, and Buddy zipped off to meet up with another bunch of dogs, over by the wading pool. Lizzie shook her head as she watched him go. Buddy really was such a good dog. Even here at the dog park, with so many wonderful distractions, he came to her when she called.

Lizzie loved the dog park almost as much as Buddy did. She loved watching all the different dogs play together. There were big ones and small ones, shy dogs and outgoing pups—and they all seemed to get along. Their owners were interesting, too. There were young couples, and older people, and sometimes a mom or dad who was juggling kids and dogs, running from the playground to the dog park and back again.

Why didn't she come more often? Lizzie usually only went to the dog park when she had a foster puppy who needed some extra socialization—that is, a puppy who needed to learn how to get along with other dogs and people.

Lizzie's family, the Petersons, were a foster family for puppies who needed homes. They took each one in just for a little while, until they could find the perfect home for that puppy. Every puppy was different, and Lizzie loved getting to know them and figuring out what type of home would be best.

With most puppies, it was enough to stay home and play with Buddy in the Petersons' fenced yard. Buddy had started out as a foster puppy, but he'd ended up being a permanent part of the family. Now, along with Lizzie's younger brothers

Charles and the Bean, Buddy helped each new foster puppy feel at home. He was always friendly and welcoming; always ready to share his toys, his treats, and his family.

ABOUT THE AUTHOR

Ellen Miles loves dogs, which is why she has a great time writing the Puppy Place books. And guess what? She loves cats, too! (In fact, her very first pet was a beautiful tortoiseshell cat named Jenny.) That's why she came up with the Kitty Corner series. Ellen lives in Vermont and loves to be outdoors with her dog, Zipper, every day, walking, biking, skiing, or swimming, depending on the season. She also loves to read, cook, explore her beautiful state, play with dogs, and hang out with friends and family.

Visit Ellen at ellenmiles.net.